MW01247863

Yu'Pik's Tale

The Dance

e.a. halper

Edited by
Susan Halper Spivak

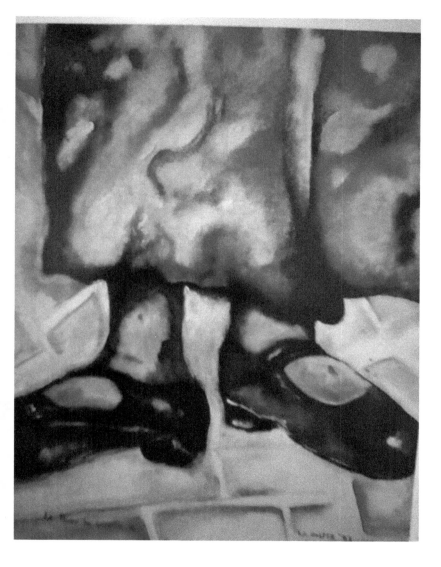

Also by e.a. halper

the entire story of biri jeet

e. (a split child)

Author's Statement

It is this author's belief that we are all entered into this world by a sexual/homosexual orientation. As we travel through the life passages and through our quintessential Universal Design, by way of choice, preference, cellular identity, or perhaps a greater fate from beyond, we become whatever we were born to be.

This book is lovingly handed over to the LGBTQIA+ Community with specious regard for who we are. Blessings to those who know who they are, and to those of us who got lost in the fray. May we all celebrate the day with pride when all of us no longer have to come from the shadows and can stand tall in the sun. Lesson finally learned: No one can take away our memory, nor our identity. Our power is within our life drive and our cellular memories. Our lives remain an embodiment of whom we were always meant to be.

Blessings.

Prologue

To those who read these words: a roadmap to guide you through the forthcoming journey.

These are the writings of the author about the many Innocents, including herself, who were not only excoriated, but also decimated by a process of conversion therapy. This was a common practice among the psychiatrists of the 60s and 70s perpetrated against the LGBTQIA+ Community, and it is well documented within their medical journals. This "therapy" was hidden under the guise of rehabilitation. How it was done, and is still being done, is what the author continuously struggles to resolve.

The author's sole purpose in writing this book is to expose the dark practices that were carried out under the cloak of psychiatric care as referenced in the <u>Diagnostic, Statistical</u> <u>Manual</u> # 3 of the day. Although removed as a guideline for treating this illness in 1973, many psychiatrists continued, and still continue today, to use these methods to control and ultimately remove this "scourge" within society.

How many Innocents still have no memory of what was done to them? These penned writings are presented to you in the format of a dark faery tale and remain only as an exposé to educate you, the general public, and those within the LGBTQIA+ Community who believe this never goes on. It did. It does. You need to be aware.

These practices present as an obsolete, maniacal process utilizing hypnotic trance, humiliation, shaming, operant and classical conditioning, analytical processes, memory blocking, hypnotic suggestion, and thought implantation. These methods would ultimately lead to the subsequent removal of the patient's sexual orientation and identity, which were then placed deep into the dark recesses of the unconscious mind of the unsuspecting patients. This author underwent this process beginning in the early 1970s and continued through 1996, with resulting after effects lasting well into the present. She has spent the last year analyzing these trace memories that now result in a dichotomy within her psyche.

The first type of memory is linear, and is based on realistic memories left unblocked by the original analyst. The second type of memory represents itself within the author's mind only as a veiled and shadowed dark miscreant Voice that is devoid of visual presence. It has been noted in medical journals that long term hypnotic trance can be causative of a false belying memory resulting in possible fantasy. This author wants the reader to know that the shadows and veiled memories may, in fact, appear real, but may in actuality, be a resulting symptom of the long-term hypnotic treatment. As a professional, the analyst needed to be aware of the ethical and moral long-term results that continue to damage and confound the decisive memories of this author. Current analytic support and treatment indicate that there may never be a resolution to the dichotomy of memory and the ability to understand what is real and what is not. This author continues, nevertheless, to congeal and reveal her original memory and identity in a logical and coherent manner.

For thirty years, a frustrating journey ensued, as this author went from one psychiatrist to another, in an attempt to find just one doctor who would listen. Instead, serious and damaging labels were bandied about with no help from any professional. Whether by fate or divine intervention, a compassionate, patient, and most distinctive therapeutic counselor appeared on the journey, bringing what was most needed: a path to healing, a healing from the damage caused by unprofessionalism and a treatment representative of a most vitriolic narcissism. Still unable to tease out which memories are real, and which are veiled from the long-term hypnosis, the fact remains, a coercion and a conversion were done. This author's therapeutic counselor believed at that time that there may never be a separation of the reality from the shadow. This counselor asked this author, "Why can't the truth rest within the entire questioning dichotomy, being both veiled and truth?" So, in the name of commitment, compassion, and decency, this author continues her healing journey in this vein.

This work remains a social commentary which is not easily understood. The author wishes to alert those who are unaware and overly trusting of the care given to the LGBTQIA+ Community that differing treatments were perpetrated and cut with rife and malfeasance that sought to take away their sexual orientation. This story continues to read as a horrific nightmare perpetrated against many Innocents in the name of healing medicine. THIS TYPE OF HEALING BORE NO SOUL.

The author wishes to share that she was in analytic treatment for fifteen years, which developed into a underlying process of coercion, aversion and conversion treatments lasting into most of her adult life. With the support of a therapeutic counselor and others, the trace memories have now begun to congeal, and this book could be processed. This author asks you to meander through the back pages toward the healing, and she even asks for your understanding. Once again, you are being asked to look at an alternative treatment that caused many suicides and many people to wear the albatross of shame about their sexuality. This treatment destroyed many innocent homosexuals, male and female, bisexuals, transgenders and queers.

This tale of cunning curiosity is hereby given to you, the reader, to make of it what you will.

You are now given access to **Yu'pik's Tale: The Dance.**

This work is dedicated to the memory of Richard Tanke, who, during the Rifkin/Quitkin Prolixin Medication Experiments at The Aftercare Program in LIJ Hillside Psychiatric Medical Center, gave up the fight and took his life. These experiments were performed, at that time, as a way of controlling the perceived psychiatric symptomology. Major psychiatric diagnoses were given to those who differed from the mores of the time. These individuals were over prescribed psychotropic and anti–psychotic medications, as well as shock treatments, in order to "dumb them down" and to control their sexual orientation. The question remains, how many more eventually took their lives because of this obsolete practice to control their sexual orientation? The following written words are mindfully dedicated to Richard Tanke, to all those who lost the battle, and to those who are still fighting it.

Dorothy Lowery, my friend, I hear you beseeching me through the Winds of Time to dedicate this book specifically to Richard Tanke and to all the rest of us who fought, and are still fighting, this battle of conversion treatments.

For those who are no longer with us, RIP

In Special Regard for my friend Ruth Dowling Bruun, MD

Throughout the lifetime of years, I have come to know you and have learned how devoted you have remained to me. I place this Wreath of Honor before you.

Your special love for all sentient beings has moved my life forward in a direction of understanding, true compassion, and dedication that does not falter.

As I have learned from your devotion to all things, humanist and sentient, I do hope my love and sentiments reach deeply into your heart, as your kindness has most certainly touched my soul.

You remain my dear friend in this life... and to you I extend a heartfelt thank you that will always hold me to a higher love for all living beings.

Stay blessed, Dr. Bruun. Your soul means much to my life... your encouragement continually moves me forward.

I love you.

Acknowledgements

Thank you to Martin Luther King for his understanding and teachings and all that is of the light and dark... "Injustice anywhere is a threat to justice everywhere."

After leaving the analytic conversion treatment, this author found her way into a beneficial treatment with a doctor of the mind, Dr. Ruth Dowling Bruun. This author presented Dr. Bruun with her confusion as to where her memories had gone during those fifteen years of analytic treatment. Dr. Bruun recognized that something most questionable had taken place. As a member of the medical ethics committee, she sought to obtain the entire fifteen years of recorded analytic treatment. This attempt was unsuccessful, as no analytic records were ever forthcoming. In the attempt to therapeutically quell the angst, she spoke most wisely, teaching me, "Memory is, at best, subjective. It is never objective. I do not know if we will ever uncover what transpired." With this in mind, she reminded this author that memory is only a perception and cannot be held as truth. The most important direction in life is only that we travel forward. To this day, as we have both aged in knowledge and time, Dr. Bruun remains my mentor and confidante in this life. I love you, Dr. Bruun.

To Dr. T: In my book, much is given to Dr. T as T'izm for the continuation of this healing journey. Although our path changed and was altered, I will never take away from her what rightfully belongs to her original intentions and levels of beginning dedication and compassion. She listened as she began a lengthy healing process that has not yet come to fruition. It was left for those who are now to be named The Others. For you, Dr. T, you know how special you were to me, and I thank you from my heart.

To Robert Paul Przybylowicz, Jr.: My heartfelt thanks for bringing this book back to life after my computer crashed and burned. I am eternally grateful to you for going a greater distance for me than anyone had done at that time.

To Cherie Honigberg, the first person to read my story. Thank you for your thought-provoking commentary and considerations reflecting the story line of this book.

To Teresa Campani, you have always watched over me since we met in college in 1968. Throughout the years, you have protected me as my symbolic big sister and helped to maintain my focus on my creativity. You remain a source of encouragement in my life, as you continue to prod me to garner my life force and to make a difference in society with my writing. Your belief in my skills makes me stronger when I am weak.

To Marge Faillace Bruce, my first Student Supervisor. You taught me a most paramount lesson which I have taken with me throughout my life which is to always remember that when working with the mentally challenged, it is essential to maintain the focus that the goal for healing is not our goal as a professional, but the goal that the client seeks for themselves on whatever level they choose. This courtesy was never offered to me in my own analytic treatment. You have recently returned to my life and continue to reinforce this lesson during our discussions. Thank you for being one of my most significant mentors.

To Phyllis Levine. How artfully you have traveled the time-honored path by my side, from the beginnings of our creative collaborations from the age of 17 to the present. To this day, we continue to create a new dream for a new school of art, delving into the absurdities of life. You remain my muse, that driving force, closest to my spirit, soul, and artistic being.

To Deborah Woodard, my night owl, who has been most supportive, not only within the realm of her poetic acumen, but her deeper understanding of what drives my inner psyche. You continue to mentor me with my literary endeavors, and I remain much appreciative of our late-night sessions, which help unlock my ability to write. I thank you.

To Candace Good, you are my friend. There are no living words to describe the true meaning of a friend. You remain undefined and solely, yet singularly, my only dance buddy in this life.

To the two Kates, who seemed to have culminated together at a time when there was a universal confusion as to which Kate became which Kate, as they appeared in the same time frame during the encryptions of this written text. But for you, my Kate Thornton, whom I love with great respect and admiration, I have always felt your soldiered protection from my living adversaries. For you, Kate, I thank you from my soul for being my guard throughout the darkness. You have brought me peace when there was no peace, and saved my life many times. You solemnly slaughtered my enemies. How important you have become to me!!! How much I love you.

And to my Kate Reavis, you appeared after I wrote the Epoch Complete, a most mysterious awakening and a foretelling. As in this story, you met me on the path and led me into a new lesbian life journey. You steadily gave me solace and showed me the way toward the altered path, telling me NOT to fear it, but to embrace it. When I asked you, you never questioned the alternative; you became my spiritual mentor. For you Kate, I thank you from my heart.

For both these Kates, as you showed me the independent journey, without judging my inequities, you have brought my life a new and meaningful dance step forward, yet sometimes backwards, but always in step with the dance called Life. Thank you.

For Hilary Flint, allow me to state that you alone personify the woman portal to my future. The compassion and wisdom that you have exhibited are far beyond your years. You will do the world a great service. I know this. Not all about how you arrived in my life, or how you left my life, will ever be fully understood. But, I am forever grateful and I promise to keep your wise teachings within my soul.

To Dr. Brooke Livingston. Patiently and carefully, you listen to my fears as you honor your oath of medicine and healing service. I owe you much, as many others before you decided to walk away. You remain by my side and continue to teach me how it is to care for a broken spirit. How special you are to me.

To Jasyn Griffith of Peace Counseling Center. Thanking you for all the dances that took place in the lobby of the Counseling Center. As if you knew all along, you brought me solace and a safe space to heal. How did you do that? Were they not just dance steps? I could never forget you. You have brought Peace to so many...

To Xavier Diamond AKA Mikki Sims, my Drag King Extraordinaire. For getting all this, and for being my special confidant, as you now become a Being who will bring forth the new order... You are ONE of the Others who has emanated from a hologram from a new - ordered seed of healing. You are my Drag King who brought me a new beginning. How do I say it, "Love you buddy?" I guess I just did.

To Jen, my publisher: Thanking you in deepest family regard. We surely placed each other into struggles beyond all that was of a necessity... I love you for all that you are and all that you will continue to do in this life. May you become all the Universe has bequeathed for you.

And with specious love for my sister, Susan Halper Spivak, for your timeless patience and wherewithal within these detailed preparations set before you. You have recently returned to my life and have stayed by my side, solely interpreting the confused language of my soul. This is the heart of a true teacher and giver of knowledge unto the world. Without you, I could not have completed this book. I love you with my heart. After all of our sibling struggles, we now see a forging relationship that makes us a family again. For whatever Earthly reasons there may be, we have left each other on that stayed yet broken, cobbled roadway, along many, many times...It is forgiven by Powers far beyond what we may ever know and far more important than our worldly misgivings. Always, Sue, for the better and for the worst of it all...e.

The cover photo, "Le Poids de Gertrude," was painted by e.a. halper in the year 2003 as an homage to Gertrude Stein.

So, it remains that without compassion, there can be no healing.

In Remembrance of Joan P. Ripp

The love poems I never wrote you... I feel silently aware... My heart is crying for the best part of me who passed away... lonely. Oh, how I miss you... My Heart... Not God nor human can fill the emptiness left when you went home... You were my anchor come hither on a whisper... given to me in my night's timeless and sleepless hearing heart... and resting within my mind's eye now... My love... my broken heart... my beloved partner in life and now beyond... you were my gentle love... I just cannot... That night before you died... you danced in the kitchen. You made me laugh... you were so frail... I longed to hold you and keep you safe forever... Ahh, but here we are separated by time... incomplete... it matters... I loved you in that one moment forever in my soul... still so fragile... so funny... so alone with me... How did you ever do it? You took my breath clearly away.

Foreword

The tale begins. Peering through a window, the sun was lower in the sky, more than usual on this day, and yet, so noticeable, was the autumnal falling of the leaves, crackling and languishing as they made their way toward the solitary ground in a manner almost mad with envy. It spoke in whispers of pride that after the deluge, there was going to be a new beginning. The monster was gone. Had it not been foretold, when the Mystic T'izm had arrived from the stars and she began the healing, that her sacred writings would now open a beginning page in the "Book of Life."

T'izm would begin a revelation and a sizing up of those mysteries that would transpire and move Yu'pik forward. And so, this tale was forming and newly fomenting. It would be shared by the Elders, as it careened and wafted, gently whispering throughout the Winds of Time. A written word for the ages now, as mighty as bolted lightning, within the stillness of the air would take its own time and would eventually be encrypted.

From the writings of the Mystic, and from the far reaches of the Heavens, she would be named herein, and to be known only as T'izm. She was sent by the Powers Above to assist on this Earth and bring the beginning of peace to a seemingly insignificant one, to be named only here as the tiny Yu'pik.

And as Yu'pik waffled her way through the darkened years, and then came thundering down from these ancient pithy pages, bowing and bending within the night, T'izm carefully opened her Books of Time and foretold a story about a legend of a one, so seemingly minute and insignificant being.

Now, an unwritten legend begins, and writes itself as a tale of one small but significant time walker herself, who, though blinded by some fierce and never-ending strikes of malfeasance, came to be known as our tiny Yu'pik.

As this tale unfolds in singular epithets, it foretells the story about a female being who battled a monstrous Voice within her own stormy world that would be finally eradicated.

On the whispers of the winds, the story of one very, very, tiny being, small in stature, but not in glory, is now given unto you, the reader, and only to be known from this day forward as **Yu'pik's Tale: The Dance.**

Epoch One: In the Beginning

As it happens, every story has a beginning. And so too, this is the beginning of a mythological, fictive allegory which has been carefully guarded for many epochs in time, and watched over by the magical being, who in these words of ancient Lore, shall be called Hillary Hers't. It is presented to you as a dark faery tale. You, the reader, will note that Hillary will emanate from a hologram at a future, undisclosed time. It was she, as Guardian, who watched over these words faithfully and will now unlock them for you, the reader, to understand that something maniacal happened and may still be happening as it is being perpetrated against the community of gentle beings that struggle to identify themselves within this darkened world. This dark faery tale is now hereby presented to you as it once long ago was silenced into a format that now screams for the ancient Tome of Lore to be brought to you. These writings were written by the Mystic, T'izm, and are now presented to you, and are to be welcomed by you as she arrives from the timeless universal Powers that guide us all. These furtive histories are handed over to you most lovingly by Sustanna, the Deliverer.

In this tale, you, the reader, are introduced to the main character Yu'pik, as well as what shall be revealed as a greater mystery and perhaps a healing. You will see that Yu'pik endeavored to stand the test of time, and that she would come to free herself from the barbs of the unethical belief system perpetrated by the analysts and other psychiatric "professionals" working in the psychiatric centers of the time. One of these analysts, in particular, is herein represented as the miscreant Voice. You will be introduced to Yu'pik's sister in these pages, as she herself carries the torch in this current incarnated life, leading you, the reader, to Yu'pik's Tale. She is known as Sustanna, who was given the daunting task of bringing to you this tale of horror and gravities about Yu'pik's life to open your discerning eyes. You will also meet the maniacal, miscreant Voice... the Pissant of Evil... that represents the dark and swarthy sounds and clouded energies that perpetrate evil and would destroy the Community of the Gentle Beings of Light, those of the LGBTQIA+ Community. You will be brought into the presence of the Others who will carry us into a future time. You will be brought the being named Hillary Hers't, whose mysterious path is to guard these pages and to deliver the Diminutive Dancer, Yu'pik and all the Others from the hands and heart of the ancient Mystic T'izm. It was she, T'izm, who first listened and heard and began Yu'pik's healings as they were passed down to her from a mysterious quorum from the Heavens. T'izm notated these healings and then indicated that they be handed over to Sustanna. And finally, you will be brought into the presence of the Dr., whose arrival through the Shadows of Time represent all that the Hippocratic Oath was meant to be.

Hilary has broken the locks and has opened the ancient crypts that she no longer guards. You, the reader, are being given the story not only of the Mystic T'izm, but also of all those Others who are enshrined within the encryptions of this tale. Follow Yu'pik's journey and how it is now placed quixotically before you to cherish within these mysterious pages of noted Lore about how the miscreant Voice tried to take away an innocence borne reality and attempted to destroy a gentle people of compassionate worth.

Heretofore, it is with honor you are presented all these epochs of time in hopes that you take this tale into your heart, as you carefully read each tattered page of angst and love with a greater compassion. YOU, THE READER, ARE REQUESTED NOW TO LEND YOUR UNDIVIDED ATTENTION AND ARDENT AUDIENCE TO THESE FACTS.

So now, from some of the recorded earthly writings of T'izm, you, the reader, are now given a story of chance and healing, relying only on the Fates and the archetypal mappings of a saving grace, the notations from one Mystic named T'izm.

The beginning...

Epoch Two: The Family, Yu'pik and Sustanna

How Yu'pik entered into this plain of existence and came to be known as the diminutive dancer

To hear our Yu'pik tell the beginnings of her entrance into this realm of existence, you must bear in mind that this One was brought in on a whirlwind of the creation of an Inuit dance, reminiscent not unlike a dance of peace and war.

Yu'pik's deliverance was of a family type. The family consisted only of two. They were sisters, but not of the blood relation type. Yu'pik's older sister, whose name was entered into the recorded Map of Life as Sustanna, was neither born into a most formal family existence, nor was she of a relation that could be deemed in any way to avoid these Fates. Yes, she was related, but not of the blood type, but just related to Yu'pik. You see, Sustanna has her own unique story, but it is not to be divulged herein. ALL ONE NEEDS TO KNOW is that Sustanna was left on the doorstep in a woven basket and was abandoned by gypsies. Not much is known about Sustanna other than it was recorded that she, and she alone, was Yu'pik's earthly sister. (ENTERED

HERE, IN THIS LIFE, AS A STRANGER OF VERY STRANGE
DESIGN, AS TOO, WAS OUR YU'PIK.) Further mention of
Sustanna will remain as fodder right now for your engaging
imagination, as the notations of T'izm are herein relayed, as they
were duly penned in a most timely manner. Hereby left for your
discretion and for the reader to understand, is how the diminutive, tiny Dancer passed on to the Mystic known as T'izm, her
own entrance into this Roadmap of the Ancient Revelations.

You see, to hear Yu'pik tell her story, she was from the
Immaculata. Neither was she blood related to the one who had
arrived prior on the doorstep (named only as Sustanna, and here
it bears repeating, she too was of an odd plumage.) However, she
arrived, as was foretold by the 1% Inuit prophesies, that one very
eccentric, yet entirely different child, would arrive in a whirlwind one day and would be of the Immaculate type (with no
parentage and no blood relations). So be it…

By this time, the very diminutive Yu'pik was heard to tell T'izm,
and she believed every word to be so that she spoke to T'izm, her
potential Healer from the beginnings of time, that she was
brought here for Immaculate reasons. (T'izm scratched her forehead but wrote it down anyway.)

As you remember, T'izm was entered into the recorded Book of
All Beings after a much-deliberated attempt by the Powers that
Be to begin the healing not only of Yu'pik but also all those
others that had been destroyed as a direct consequential dark
effort by the corrupt and foul Voice of malfeasance.

Yu'pik believed herself to be one great dancer and thought she
could create great changes within the world, as she devoted her
steps and deliverance of her dance as she knew it to be. T'izm
was heard to say, "Healings are somewhat likened to a dance,

some steps forward, others back, Yu'pik." So, Yu'pik accomplished the beginnings of her healing by way of learning an old English board game called Balderdash. The steps of her dance were always similar to how the rules of nonsense (one of Yu'pik's fond yearnings and leanings in life) would be played out. These steps were never dissimilar to the steps of the fancier footwork of The Dance. But let it be known, Yu'pik, born in a whirlwind of a 1% Inuit war and peace, a dance from whence she emanated on the new horizon. Yu'pik never, ever knew how to dance, nor did she ever know how to carry a rhythm. Yu'pik never could, and thus, as she told T'izm after the healings began to happen, she came crashing into this world because she just could not. T'izm was about to learn all this, as from afar she took note. (T'izm scratched her forehead again. She really did.)

Addendum to Epoch Two

So, as it was, T'izm was a very ancient soul who had been around since the beginning of time. She was called back into the Records of Time (which is of an endless and beginningless iconoclastic ideology.) As it was deemed, she was the one called on to manage this great cataclysm, begging the beginnings of the new world order. T'izm was of a mindset to be one very old soul. So, when it was predestined for her to enter into our little Yu'pik's decimated and unidentifiable life, she appeared as a much younger soul than our Yu'pik. T'izm came into Yu'pik's side of existence at a time when Yu'pik was much older than T'izm. T'izm was always much more manipulative and much craftier than the diminutive dancer, who could neither dance, nor could she do much of anything anymore, by the time T'izm was to arrive. HOWEVER, T'izm was always there. She had always been there, dedicated to journeys, taking note and yes, scratching her forehead, and wondering. All you need to know is T'izm was just beginning to be wondering, "What am I doing here?" And The Powers that Be wondered, "Would T'izm ever be able to deliver?"

So here you have it, the very opening introductions of our Yu'pik and her sister named Sustanna.

And herein also begins the next of the notations, detailed fastidiously by T'izm, of the story now marking our Yu'pik's female friends. These friends, of homosexual nature, were what caused the void and plethoric all controlling Voice to use its contemptible power to destroy our Yu'pik's, and possibly many others', identity and their intellectual capacity. This destruction rendered by the Voice and others like the Voice, acting in the name of Conversion and Mind Control, would bring about the obsolescence and non- existence of the beings. It became the causation into further finding the answers, begging a need to be answered in time. And so, a tale was being written, devised and taken note by the one known as the Mystic, named T'izm.

As T'izm relates here for you the next epoch detailing the friends of Yu'pik, the ones of the female type, you are hereby introduced to those who shall be called the Friends of Constancy. The first consistent one, recorded in T'izm's notations, named only as Devorak, as well as the Group… of 2,566, are hereby presented unto you. Devorak, part of the Group of 2,566, having heard her name whispered on the wind, at this point in time, looked upward, gave a big sigh, and went off to meditate.

To be noted, Yu'pik was gathered into this life, predisposed, and predestined also, to enter into a Healing Contract with the one known as T'izm. The notations therefore continue, as penned by T'izm, thus for your understanding and clarity of mindset, in knowing what is known and what is not known, and how it is that the dark chased the light. But the light will always consume the darkness. The tale continues in a quagmire, a sort of board game, Quixotically, so to speak, otherwise known as Balderdash. This game requires the players merely to make up statements designed to fool the other players. The one who fools the most players wins. According to the rules of the game, you are hereby given permission to take another step forward, a Dance Step forward, and the expression of the emotion, herein involved, brings forth a rhythm and movement of the body in preparation for exuberant joys. (All that in the life of Yu'pik, all this was missing and most forgotten. But remember, Yu'pik never instinctively knew how to dance at all, but had a burning, willing desire to become a great dancer.)

So, the diminutive one and her Friends of Constancy within this faery tale are revealed here to queue up your imagination, which will become an emotional engagement of sorts. You will be asked to join in and bandy about in a rousing, rhythmic balancing act.

With a bit of nonsense, this tale is carried forward. Here is a mystery for you, the reader, ready to unfold... a story, a board game, a dance in life, that in finality, results in a 1% Inuit Immaculata revelation.

The mystery of what was perpetrated by the Voice has deeply scarred the hearts of the many who live within its plight. The Voice's great eradication, meant to remain a mystery, attempted to destroy the homosexual beings within. NEVER AN ANSWER...

The one defining result that would emerge, created by way of some nonsense perhaps, or something called logic, would become Yu'pik's Dance.

Epoch Three: The Female Friends of Constancy

The Attractions… the Conversions… and the Aversions

When Yu'pik was very young, she had a companion. This blonde female was not unlike the birds that arrive in a smile and a timely flight in the Spring, allowing these sentient beings to sprint about. This female being brought new hope after the dismally long, lonely childhood winter months, as our Yu'pik was becoming unto herself, and here this being, that the tiny Dancer first laid eyes on, and cared for so lovingly, had a name. Her name is lovingly entered into the time-honored Archives of Life, and **just now** remembered as the one who first stole the diminutive one's heartstrings. So too, her name will be lovingly remembered as Robin, much like the beings of light, the harbingers of the green new growth of life and warmth of the sun in the Spring.

It is now understood that Robin, not Devorak, was indeed the first of the 2,566 friends that would begin to appear in Yupik's life. In Numerological teachings, as recorded within the Akashic Records within the Heavens, the number 2,566 becomes the

Number One, the very first of all numbers. It puts power directly in our hands as a symbol of independence, confidence, and new beginnings. Robin was the first, and as the tethering Voice of evil said, "No, these feelings cannot be, they are of the unnatural type." Robin, Yu'pik's first heart, was to become immersed in a stone wall of silence, eventually in our Yu'pik's unconscious mind. Yu'pik would not be allowed to remember her heart beatings for this female friend, known as Robin, the One she stole her first kiss from, and her first feelings of other worldly love. Robin was taken from the conscious memory of the tiny Dancer. As it was now happening. Yu'pik was being made null and void and placed into a most controllable and probable state of being, where no longer... could she... would she... and now she just could not... never again just be.

But the analyst, herein presented as the Voice, never considered the alternative. There was no differing position to take, and, blinded by that indifference and great bias, she was unable to see what she had never planned, that those greater universal Powers that Be would re-write Yu'pik's story. One cannot understand Heaven or Hell if you know nothing of life. It now became her own egotistical, vitriolic, narcissistic feat, so overpowering that she never suspected, nor never knew, anything of the called upon arrival of the Mystic, T'izm. She never counted on a counterattack from the Heavens beyond. She only knew that Yu'pik's identity was to be eradicated and separated from her being and that she was to be washed of her memories. It would be a slow process which would be perpetrated and self-reinforced during the next fifteen years through thought implants, hypnotic suggestions, re-programming, classical conditioning, acts of shaming and humiliation and all the aversion treatments. Thus, the new behaviors would be formed, then learned, and then placed in a self-reinforced patterning of behavior.

Over many tedious years that bore Yu'pik great pain, anytime she dared think or mention any of her heart beatings for her female friends, a most sinister process was instituted and was perpetrated upon our Yu'pik. Unbeknownst to her, and done by way of trickery, misrepresentation, and great evil manipulations forced upon the Dancer, it was formulated in the darkness of night, and a concluding consternation by behavioral modifications. The buried memory now revealed itself as a veiled and shadowed voice of great darkness. Many posthypnotic suggestions, only known to the darkness as the Voice, began to filter into Yu'pik's unconscious mind, formulating a new conscious identity.

Yu'pik was taught to be Pavlov's dog. SHE WAS TAUGHT TO BE A TRAINED DOG. So, at only a sound, and a reward, or a semblance of a demeaning, shameful, vitriolic punishment, Yu'pik was able to be controlled. This was the crux of the classical conditioning utilized by the Voice. As with Pavlov's dogs, the Voice used pleasing rewards accepted by the patient. In Yu'pik's case, she used the reward of memory and feeling of sexual pleasures as she rebuilt her Ego. Perhaps by a clicking sound, maybe a visual projection told in stale stories by the veiled and evil Voice, that would put Yu'pik into a very deep trance, Yu'pik, would be by now, unable to remember that she had even once dreamed to be a dancer and a great entertainer). But the point here is... IT WAS HER DREAM... and it was TAKEN from her through the repetitious reinforcement of mind control, in the dark of night, because the Voice needed to have total control over our Yu'pik's life, identity, and orientation.

Yu'pik had a total of 2,566 female friends totaling in spiritual numeric numerology equal to the number 1. (Remember, the number 1 in the recordings of Spiritual Numerology represent the Powers that the Heavens hold over each and every one of us, and that these Powers combined, represent the energy of all darkness and light.) T'izm understood what MLK said best, "Were it not for the darkness, one could never see the stars."

Time was at hand. Some of the names garnered by T'izm during the healing remain intact now, after many years of being suppressed. These names began to resurface from deep within Yu'pik's unconscious. (Notated and named herein for you to see from the documentations of T'izm are some of the names of import)... Sally P, Joanna G, Barbara H, Christine F, Roben D and finally Robin E. The relationships with these women were completely annihilated and removed from Yu'pik's entire memory by the Voice. These were the beginnings of the coercion treatments of brainwashing and caused Yu'pik to become forgetful during these fifteen years. It was important for the Voice to erase the memory of these women and remove them from Yu'pik's entire life existence in order to complete her conversion. And finally, Yu'pik's life partner and soul mate, Joan, who ended her life because Yu'pik could no longer be intimate with her. The Voice had succeeded again in eradicating all sensations of touch from any woman. The reader is asked to understand that by this time, Yu'pik's entire identity and sexual orientation had been annihilated by the evil Voice. It bears mentioning here, in great sadness, but yet in deep love, that this final evil caused Joan to take her life resulting from an unfulfilled relationship. If Yu'pik could have, she would have. But she did not yet have insight into what had transpired from the darkened commands of the evil Voice. Could there have been a resolve without Joan's painful solution? Yu'pik's regret will always remain paramount, because she loved Joan so deeply. Yu'pik was heard to lament, "I am so sorry that the truth was hidden from us. Rest in Peace my Heart."

And then T'izm's voice was heard to be whispering through the Winds of Time in an attempt to console our Yu'pik, "Not everything in life has an answer. Some things must be held within our soul merely as a reminder of our own human frailty. There are times we must carry the pain." All those female beings (our want-to-be dancer loved and cared for them all) had been blocked from her memory in one way or another by the evil Voice. What is now known, Yu'pik has no memory of, and has no mention of, any of them in her daily existence, except for Joan. As these names were beginning to resurface, T'izm scratched her forehead and took note.

T'izm had been careful to note these beings of inexpressible warmth, that Yu'pik held within her heart beatings, as they began to emerge from the deadly depths and realms of her unconscious. Most remain within the stifling darkness, lost, and are still needing to be revealed. But Yu'pik can still see their faces within her mind's eye and wonders what the names are of these ghosted beings. As T'izm began to understand the storyline, she noted the names. She understood the horror and the nightmare. It was up to T'izm to undo the unforgivable and heal the wounds and scars left by the darkness. T'IZM WAS ON TO IT AND WAS READY TO GET THE TASK DELIVERED from so many eons prior, as it had been written in the recorded Book of Beings of Light and Darkness. Yu'pik was beginning to find herself in a great amount of reverence for what T'izm was attempting to accomplish. Would T'izm be able to accomplish this formidable task? Even though she was sure at times, she was not sure about much these days. She scratched her forehead and continued to take notations. T'izm took scrupulous notations and was sure to note each detail. Within T'izm's makeup was the inherent ability to heal great misgivings in all of Time. T'izm, in fact, remains a compassionate being. As it is written in the Book of Life, "There will be none other like this One at any other given time, but there will be others to follow." Her skills were honed by a greater Being, a GOD, greater than anyone could know. Yu'pik was about to be delivered after many, many years of silence and pain.

This Mystic now appeared as their pre-ordained meeting was about to take place.

These female friends remain of great import because the mindset that the great evil Voice held was that all homosexual leanings must be devoured and rendered obsolete at all costs. The Voice also believed that homosexuality was abnormal. Yu'pik believed that was wrong. It was just outright and purely proven to be wrong, as many Innocents were devoured in those days. These were the Innocents who loved women, were women, and were loved by women. (Some were of the male orientation also, but not mentioned in any detail here, because that remains for another time.)

One can only wonder and consider this sanctimonious amplitude of wrongdoing. It was thought to be a superior belief in a system of totality. That was just wrong... IT WAS WRONG... IT BORE NO SOUL.

Epoch Four: The Conversion...Born From the Ashes and Death of the Miscreant Evil Voice

IT WAS MANY YEARS LATER. T'izm had made her timely appearance by now and was tirelessly attempting to gain the tiny Yu'pik's trust. (THOUGH OUR TINY DANCER WAS NOT ABLE TO DO MUCH TO BRING THIS TO FRUITION.) But miracles sometimes do happen. Here it is, how T'izm and Yu'pik developed the doorway to the remembrance of the frozen, blocked memories (that had been placed in darkness by the evil Voice from hell.) In an indeterminate attempt to show just how the Mystic and Yu'pik began to work together in a most mean-ingful and saving way, you, the reader, are hereby given a large portion of T'izm's written passages on that one day in the life of our diminutive Dancer. The doorway is now open for you as it concerns the veracity of those blended memories in just the way they first emerged in a most confusing representation of trace memories. Those memories that emanated on this day reveal the DARK ROOM OF CONVERSION THAT STOLE THE LIVING BREATH FROM MANY INNOCENTS INCLUSIVE OF OUR YU'PIK.

Yupik had just finished her day in the imaginings of remembering the nightmares of the night prior. Today she would have to spend an hour again, confessing those wild imaginings and half-truths to the One named T'izm, who had just recently arrived. Yu'pik was forcing the thoughts to back down, but T'izm's powers were stronger. Yu'pik's locked memories were emerging and converging with her conscious thoughts. T'izm was patient. The re-emergence was happening, and this is how it transpired. Was it something that happened this hour in the morning, or was it so late in the day? Yu'pik had no real idea just what time it was. Our Yu'pik started overflowing in the trace beginnings of partial memories. They did, however, represent the entire darkness and what had happened to cause the total loss of Yu'pik's identity and memories. Yu'pik kept initiating a pushback, but now to no avail. Compassion HAD BEGUN TO WIN. Yu'pik could not contain this healing. She was fearful. The Voice had modified her persona to believe she was meaningless, and her thoughts were mere facets of sick imaginings and delusional, dangerous beliefs. Yu'pik had no trust in herself, nor did she know who she really was anymore. She did not trust this One known as T'izm. Surely, she was the same as all the ones from the darkness. Yu'pik felt attached to T'izm, who was able to utilize this attachment, and T'izm was able to then empower the beginnings of the Healing and Saving Grace. So, the thoughts eked out of Yu'pik's very consciousness. It was all so difficult to discuss. Yu'pik let it drop a bit as it floated away, but to no use. T'izm's power of compassion was stronger than anything our tiny Dancer really could fathom. Remember, T'izm's powers of healing began strong and other worldly from a time prior to this. But could she be counted on to deliver?

The first trace memory emerged. It was Yu'pik speaking in broken words, because she no longer had language. She was unable, she could no longer, she just could not. Intangible words emerged... "wishing for a cigarette..." Then the darkness spoke and determined... "Yu'pik, you could be used, and these cigarette cravings could be used, to block many thoughts and works... I can take you over in this way..." Yu'pik sat motionless and helpless, fighting internally, being imprisoned, unable and mostly frozen. (YOU, THE READER, MUST TRY TO UNDERSTAND WHAT IT IS LIKE TO BE FROZEN IN SPACE AND TIME.) And so, it became a fact, and so it happened, through trance and posthypnotic suggestion, through fears and humiliations... our tiny Dancer became blocked of every thought through her cravings and addiction to cigarettes. Yes, Yu'pik was altered. Every thought and every dream she ever held for her own was now gone.

Yu'pik now found herself drawn to telling T'izm, her newly found confessor, the very strange beginnings of the conversion. Strange and nocturnal happenings and remembrances pushing forth from out her unconscious mind were emerging, those of spirits and ghosts and other things that scream in the night. Yu'pik felt an odd and peculiar sense and sensitivity about this T'izm. So, T'izm's powers were strong and now through this relaying of all these trace memories that seemed only crazy and a huge embarrassment to Yu'pik, a healing vision was developing. Sometimes as confessor, oft times though, through this identity of the Mystic, where Yu'pik found herself drawn into T'izm's web of compassion, Yu'pik began to tell T'izm and reveal those darkest sins and misdeeds wrought with rife and catastrophic situations perpetrated against our Dancer. The thoughts she had been convinced were crazy, the thoughts she had grown to believe were symptoms of a labeled and much greater illness and were part and parcel to only the delusions, were falling away.

Back to the memories now, where the evil voice held our Dancer within the confinement by the darker and darkest mesmerizing Voice. (A TYPE OF STOCKHOLM SYNDROME WAS BEING

INITIATED TO MAINTAIN TOTAL CONTROL BY THE VOICE, IMPRISONING YU'PIK AND NOT ALLOWING HER TO ESCAPE.) "You, Yu'pik, belong to me. I alone control you. No one will know what I have accomplished here. You are my creation now. IT IS I WHO HAVE BIRTHED YOU." Yu'pik began to twitch in fear as the memories began to spill out unto the ears and compassionate being of T'izm's lengthy and miles-long distanced arm hold. Yu'pik fought for time and escape. She complained to T'izm, "My dreams and visions of these confessions are only about a frail and unhearing God. T'izm, I fear I am symptomatic and sick. DOES GOD EVER LISTEN? T'izm, He is a Divinity who never listens. He/she does not seem to care."

Yu'pik was at this time unaware that T'izm had been sent by way of a Great Quorum prior to Time itself, and that T'izm had become that preordained Mystic sent to clear a passage to this one named Yu'pik. T'izm spoke inside her being at this time and was taking scrupulous notations, because innately she knew the Time was now. She thoughtfully scratched her forehead in great anticipation, knowing that this albatross of mixed light and darkness, somewhere at this time... was still tightened about Yu'pik's scarred and veiny neck. "You bastard," T'izm said to herself. "You tried to choke the air from the tiny Dancer's being. I just cannot fathom the depth of this darkness." It is documented in excessive notations, underlined and denoted by quotations, that T'zim now is heard to whisper at great lengths and scratch her forehead, as she tirelessly worked to free Yu'pik from the holds of this ligature and strangulation. Yu'pik then spoke, "T'izm, I cannot have someone touch, hold or hang anything about my neck or on or about my aging body. Sometimes, it becomes a battle betwixt the dove of freedom, and ofttimes, the treacherous transferential beings I loathe. I see it, only as you, T'izm, you might be part of the evil Voice. T'izm? I CANNOT. I SEE YOU AND CONFUSE YOU, I DARE NOT

TRUST YOU." T'izm was ever so patient and thinking now again, "How could I, T'izm, get Yu'pik to not efface me as that demon?" This, T'izm realized, was up to the Powers from Beyond. This had to do with the Fates. It had to do with her own trust in Yu'pik, and Yu'pik's abilities to seize the day. Not in any way could she, T'izm, use her abilities to help herself or help Yu'pik to now make that crossover to the freedom. T'izm realized her own frailty that she was also caught in the Fates, and now too, this was up to the Fates. This would not come from her powers; however great they were. The diminutive One just could not. That was true. Those calls out to any one being in the darkened night and those silent, smothered yearnings, the screaming that reminded Yu'pik of the darkness (and Yu'pik was frightened and alone and just wanted a mother. She would cry out in her frozen state, "You all dance in fires of evil." Yu'pik only saw the evil waves of the Voice as they consumed her. But this one tiny, diminutive Dancer, who just could not, now has discovered mixed about within her mind, other thoughts, other mentions, placed there by the Voice. So no longer would Yu'pik have ANY ability to dare to call out and scream and save herself. Inwardly, Yu'pik understood this had been an ulterior plot perpetrated by the darkness, and that Voice belched forth and said, "No one will ever know what I did here." The evil Voice covered her tracks well, she thought. T'izm scratched her forehead...

Back to the meeting of minds where the two time-travelers were holding their unique existence as Mystic and victim. Yu'pik only wanted T'izm's compassion now, as she was now her confessor. (Though this was the name the Voice had our Yu'pik call HER, Yu'pik did not like this entitlement and barely used it to call out for T'izm.) Nay the less, it was beginning to happen. T'izm sensed, as Yu'pik was confessing her sins, a change of heart was transpiring that IT MUST be now. But there were times Yu'pik could not speak the words. They'd get caught in her tightened throat. These fears, T'izm sensed, could be resolved and become evolved and be healed. Maybe? (T'izm herself, was not sure. She scratched her forehead.) T'IZM KNEW THAT IN THE DANCER'S MIND, repeated and repeated, THESE FEARS OF TELLING THE DARK HAPPENINGS that did remain for long periods of tortuous times, in her mind and flesh, were ruled by the Voice. It was not to be resolved and never revealed to anyone under penalty of torture, at least not yet, but it was transpiring. The memories that Yu'pik awoke with this morning, almost preordained, as her stomach knotted deeply inside with the semi-conscious visions that were evolving into realities of yet unspoken horrors. This little being of such great consternation heard a supernatural calming voice which told her to place warmth from her own hands onto her abdomen and let the heat heal this, her own tortured being. It was true, Yu'pik's stomach was vomiting up every day, regurgitating ALL these repulsive horrors. For the first time, Yu'pik did what she thought T'izm was telling her to do. She did what she could. She did. She thought it was T'izm, maybe her spirit, but she did not know. It was a mystery. But within the shroud of this mystery, (Yu'pik did not actually know. She trusted, as she told her confessor, T'izm, "I did not know. I find the demons and visions of light mixed into one, sometimes with you, sometimes vague vision, oft times a darkness." It was true, Yu'pik could not trust. Her trust had long since been taken from her. T'izm silently prayed as Yu'pik continued to speak. "You appear to me as a spirit from my frail and empty God, but then I cower, T'izm. Could this be the trans-ferential demon I call the scathing darkness and the void of all that dwells within as only evil? Or is it you, my Mystic?"

"Monster," T'izm thought out loud and Yu'pik spoke with her in almost an orchestrated harmony, "Visions of light and darkness are twisted and shadowed in my brain. T'izm?"

It was now late in the day as the sun was sinking and so too were Yu'pik's hopes. But not so with T'izm. She gave her more time, because it was a doorway opening. "You T'izm, you called?" Yu'pik picked up the calling, relieved. T'izm worked swiftly and moved Yu'pik out from under her covers of fear. Our diminutive One could only crunch down in a stodgy chair, disgruntled. But here, Yu'pik was reduced to only a miniscule remnant of her being. New, wholesome visions were being uncovered. Yu'pik found at this time she could hide and find solace wrapped within her visions of T'izm's other-orbed, other-worldly, and heavenly robes.

T'izm recognized that the transpiring prophesies were now at hand. She recognized that Yu'pik was able to soak up her warm voice as she listened intently for the healing to take place. REMEMBER, our dear reader, these two beings had never met. T'izm quelled that torn heart from a great distance, and she expertly knew how to stave off the shadows and fears. There were other worldly boundaries which were adhered to only by the overseeing of the Powers of Light (that, ultimately, we all adhere to). T'izm instilled quietly and calmly, somehow letting Yu'pik know that she was NOT the miscreant swarthy Voice from hell's pits. AND NOW, Yu'pik made one conscious decision. (Remember, all prior ability to make any personal decision had been removed in the analytic process, thus giving the evil Voice consummate power to make Yu'pik's decisions. Yu'pik would NOT transfer this power to the Mystic, T'izm. She spoke almost from the center of another being now (T'izm knew the healing was beginning to transpire!). Yu'pik whispered, "You will be the one I call for the healing. I will smite this transference. I want a cigarette. God, I haven't wanted one in eons, T'izm. The Voice would have me smite and block you, and all who would dare to ask the questions which could cause the memories to resurface. I could have done that and turned you out. But I see you from afar, awaiting just on the other side of the time zone. Mystic, you have allowed me to make my choices. So now, I will abide. I will welcome your Light and Being." (With some trepidation, and with one tiny tear drop, Yu'pik whispered the words, "Thank you kindest Being." It emanated cautiously from Yu'pik's breath. T'izm began here to give advisement at once. She said, "No, no Yu'pik, no cigarettes." Surrounded by T'izm's unconditional graces, Yu'pik felt the compassion at once, as it pushed through the Lightwave of Time itself. T'izm continued, "The blocking must be thwarted." Our Yu'pik listened intently. HENCE, because she listened... she WAS AWARDED the semblance of a peace of mind brought by the One Healing Saving Grace, known only as unconditional regard from the One named T'izm. More memories started to emerge.

Finally, the conversion, in a flood of revelations, was beginning now to be revealed. (Generally written here, it will be openly described within the next chapter.) Yu'pik's persona had been switched through a manipulative evil feat of mesmerizing and post-hypnotic suggestions, as the voice took her identity and made Yu'pik null and void in mind and being. T'izm knew now the full extent, and she was freeing all this from Yu'pik's mind. T'izm had much work to do as the Voice eerily eked through Yu'pik's now conscious memory, "I made you believe something that was not true... Hocus Pocus."

Clearly, it had been a feat of dark magic, and great misgiving perpetrated on the tiny Dancer. T'izm knew in her heart that much work had to be done. She worried. Could she untangle this web? Was Yu'pik up to the task at hand? It became the most exhausting type of work, with no way of knowing the final outcome. It would remain a mystery. That CONVERSION had been perpetrated from the beginning, by acts of coercion and aversion, and had now been uncovered and were beginning to be set free. The miscreant Voice of Darkness, that had stolen our diminutive Dancer's identity in an act of malfeasance, was dissipating. T'izm was most aware. Yu'pik was not yet totally aware of all the facts. What WAS known, Yu'pik would soon be within the Healing Graces of the One known as T'izm.

Following is an addendum to Epoch 4, which will give you, the reader, greater detail into the ways that the malfeasance of the evil Voice delivered her blows to Yu'pik and how the Conversion transpired.

Addendum to Epoch Four: How the Conversion Transpired

It was a manipulation of the mind by the Force of Darkness.

Yu'pik's sexual orientation and persona were expressed through her identity as a woman and the idea that all women are paramount. This cellular idea was transposed through deep hypnotic trance by the dark reaches of visualization that had Yu'pik believe after many years of brainwashing and controlling humiliations, that she now bore the sexual orientation of the Dark Voice. No longer was she female identified. Yu'pik became opposed to her very own born sexual orientation. But Yu'pik was smarter. She spoke quickly as Time was of all importance now. She told herself, as the Voice was perpetrating the conversion, "No one can take your memory or your cellular identity, Yu'pik. This Voice is about to cover over your being with veils of untruth. One day, you will remember who you are. You will know that you are a great Dancer, though tiny of SPIRIT and diminutive in nature... You will return..." (It was an anticipation of what was about to transpire and a foretelling of the future. But all foretelling prophesies are never set in stone.) AND IN THIS WAY, Yupik's orientation and intellectual persona were altered, making her believe in a vision of herself that was not true. Her Id became that of the Voice. From the inception, the Voice had Yu'pik visualize the concepts of ID, EGO, and SUPER EGO. Once this was accomplished, the Voice stated, "You have become mine to manipulate, and now I have the ability to alter your entire being and take over your identity and thoughts. So now you must think only as I will have you think."

Through hypnotic trance, thought implantation, behavioral modification, operant conditioning, great humiliations and visualizations utilizing these psyche mindsets and mind control, the malfeasant Voice now owned Yu'pik's ability to think. Added to the conversion process, Yu'pik was often given psychotropic medications to control the thought process, as it was meant to do through thought blocking. In this way Yu'pik was devoid of her love for women, which the Voice had deemed unnatural. Perhaps the Voice believed she could discard these self-proclaimed perceptions forever from Yu'pik and all others like her. The Voice maniacally whispered, "My Id is now your own, and it is pressed ever so deeply through hypnotic trance way down in your unconscious, where it can never be undone." So Yu'pik was coerced to hold on to a vision that the evil Voice was able to implant, allowing her to take hold of the Dancer's Id, Ego, and Super Ego. Yu'pik's entire being and mindset became owned by the Voice. She was no longer owner of her sexual orientation and her identity. The malfeasant Voice not only took her mind, but her entire being as she said, "You will never be touched by a woman again, nor will you touch another woman. You are mine, (maniacal laughter) and I will do the same to the rest like you.) You will go henceforth and be forever changed and normalized." YU'PIK THOUGHT IN A PANIC, "This is obsolete. This is not a mind think. It is my cellular identity from birth. It is THE ESSENCE OF MY BEING."

But too little too late. Yu'pik hastily placed her memory of who she was in her thoughts, forever now to be unspoken, repeatedly resounding in her mind, to be unearthed at a much later time. (For who can really take our memories and who can take our identity?) REPEATEDLY, YUPIK'S MIND ECHOED IN A SILENT MANTRA, in a panic, in a way to save herself, OVER AND OVER, "I AM THE DIMINUTIVE DANCER AND I LOVE ALL WOMEN." This mantra was repeated UNTIL THE ONLY THING THAT YU'PIK COULD HEAR, WAS THE infiltrating sound of the EVIL VOICE, AS IT ENTERED ALL HER BRAINWAVES... ID FIRST, EGO, SUPER EGO... YU'PIK'S MANTRA WAS ANNIHILATED AND GONE.

As previously mentioned, a long time would pass before T'izm's arrival, bringing with it possibilities of hope. NO ONE EVER BELIEVED YU'PIK. SHE WAS ALWAYS GIVEN A VERY SERIOUS DIAGNOSIS. No one believed her. The time would come, and the outcomes would be altered by what would be changed in the wind by a SPIRITUAL FORECAST of GREATER LIGHT... AND TIME.

BUT TOO LATE... NOW IT WAS UP TO THE ARRIVAL OF T'IZM AND THE ABILITY OF OUR TINY DANCER TO HAVE A MEETING OF THE MINDS WITH HER YET UNKOWN, UNTRUSTED MYSTICAL BEING. Something that seemed gone and impossibly forsaken now became clear. Yu'pik was now indeterminately changed in persona, intellect and orientation until the Light would finally swing the pendulum and consume all this darkness. For some, it is known, they will never remember. Maybe a mystery. But Yu'pik was born to remember. IT WAS WRITTEN IN SOME BOOK, WASN'T IT?

Epoch Five: The Longing

For once, now alone and really alone, Yu'pik longed for her mother and her protections. Yu'pik now realized by this act of rude awakening that she was not of the immaculate type at all, nor was her sister Sustanna an orphan after all, the one left in a woven basket, abandoned on the doorstep, left by the gypsies. Yu'pik gathered all her 1% Inuit heritage and mustered up a great many tears. But Sustanna was nowhere around. She, remember, was not even to be mentioned again. So now it was up to T'izm. She must be the one to be all or nothing at all. It must be T'izm and the Others. The prophesy must be enacted and the healing must continue to take place. There was no turning back. There really was never any turning back. Fate was now in the notations and the hands of T'izm and the Universal Powers that Be.

And there came that Voice, which spoke these darkened words as an eternal reminder that evil **does** exist, "I made you believe something that was not true... Hocus Pocus."

Yupik then considered the alternative, understood intuitively, and whispered ever so resoundingly,

"Balderdash!"

Epoch Six: The Time Has Come

And as time came to pass, and many years had floated in and out of this story, and the compass of life, T'izm finally said to our Yu'pik, "Yu'pik, time has come. It is time to end the story." Yu'pik was then heard to officiously respond, but in her opposingly opposite manner, most silently and softly in an ever so cautious tone. For it must be told, Yu'pik had become somewhat and exceedingly most brazen throughout the year of the great Beginning Healing. New events were beginning to unfold here. "Oh," Yu'pik contended, "How will the ending transpire, T'izm?" And it was then, that our Yu'pik peered ever so deeply into the Mystic T'izm's ancient eyes, and seeking into her soul ever more deeply, T'izm was heard to whisper and thus spoke, "My little Yu'pik, it is time, and you know, and you do know, you cannot peer into my eyes like this." (This is one of many endings denoted through the warp in time, because nothing is ever really set in stone within the Heavens until it actually transpires.) Yu'pik then most softly said, "Oh? Why can I not peer into your eyes?" And then, as though it was flowing like a river which was right on key within the timeline, T'izm said, "Because, my little friend, (though they were not friends at all) because we have never met. I LIVE IN

Ohio and YOU LIVE IN North Carolina, and we have never seen each other throughout all these many years. COME NOW. It is time, and besides, I have merely been a figment of your imagination. And as it goes, there are boundaries." Hearing this, Yu'pik spoke a little more bravely now to her wise, mystical teacher, "My foot is tapping, T'izm."

T'izm began to engage a smile. It was beginning again. It was happening now. Once begun, a Healing could not be stopped or thwarted or even altered. And T'izm was beseeching the borders of time and the gods of all imaginings, a written word, as this was to be now all unfolding into the Book of Life. The corners of the universe and the tattered pages of the Book of Life began to echo and revolve, and stars began to engulf our two time-travelers. And yes, for the first time in many and all the troubled years, our Yu'pik started to dance. And though, through steps of trepidations and failing fears, at first, and at long last, she then took a courageous leap. And faith was at hand for the moment, roaring and grumbling through the great Inuit belly of Time. One could hear what sounded like thunder at first. But it was more than that. It was the healing sounds of T'izm, and she was LAUGHING. As you know, dear reader, Yu'pik never knew how to dance and she was beginning to look quite ridiculous. T'izm's laughter was resonating. And here, within the history and firefall of one million stars, oh yes, it must have been at least one million, T'izm was roaring with resounding bouts of laughter as Yu'pik was at first tenuously beginning to waltz. She then danced her way by bounding leaps. And as her tiny toes officiated the tapping, she found her way into the annals and chambers of the ancient Tomes of Lore. These Tomes were now carrying the senselessness and yet the sensitivity of time. And now as before, never together, but bonded by a greater ethereal resounding sound, if you listen closely to the winds of time and place your ear to the threshold of the opening doorstep, (of course, not the one where

Sustanna had been left) of imagination, yes, you can hear T'izm healing. And yes, laughing, and yes, she really was laughing. And you can hear the tiny diminutive Yu'pik tipping the Scales of Time with her magic feet and fancy footwork. As her tiny feet "sacheted" out the sacred dance and breakdown (a fierce rollicking dance) of the Tides of Time, both T'izm and Yu'pik laughed and danced, from one beam of starlight to each and every "Einsteinian" Passage of imaginary starlight. Forever, for the ages, you, the reader, are now given the act of the Beginning Healing. You are given the knowledge of knowing absolutely nothing. You are given your God Speed. You are given a vision of great joy and a study in compassion and love, and a great mystery of time and deliverance. You now can behold the Darkness and the Light and the fact that T'izm and Yu'pik never, ever met on this plane of existence. It is relative, but important to note, and as was spoken, it is knowing that the Healing truly began in this manner.

Let it be known that Yu'pik never knew how to dance and that T'izm understood the facets of time-honored Healing. But here is a mystery for you, dear reader… because T'izm had the ability to disappear, it was never apparent if she would ever reappear in Yu'pik's life. Hence, the story of one diminutive Dancer remains ever changing.

Epoch Seven: Epoch Complete, a Prophesy

Yu'pik gathered herself up and slowly, most hesitantly, began to put her tattered self together. She brushed and dusted off the particles of dust from the roadway, where she had been sleeping in the dirt. Yu'pik stretched and yawned. Stardust was floating upward, ethereally dissipating piecemeal into the heavens. T'izm, too, was gone.

Somewhere down toward the end of the road an old music box was playing what sounded like an older-yet Bette Midler song, emanating from a tinny record player, or maybe it was just from a craggy old juke box, "Standing at the end of the road boys, waiting for my new friends to come, I don't care if I'm hungry or cold, I got to get me some."

Then, through the wafting mixture of roadway and stardust and tinny music, through the haze, Yu'pik could barely make out what she thought was a blondish figure of... yes it was... a lone independent woman, peering through the haze and making her way toward our Yu'pik. Her name, she said, was Kate. Just Kate. (Could it be another mystery?) And, she was saying she had heard some tinny music playing off in the distance and began to follow the sounds when she spied our Yu'pik standing and dusting herself off from the stardust and the dirt. Perplexed, she considered the following. "I guess it was all just a dream." Yu'pik bent down to pick up a lone piece of glitter that looked to be shining like the letter T. She squinted at it and vaguely remembered something about some mystic Healer somewhere. She let it go, just as Kate, the independent walker, reached her. So, it was Kate who then surreptitiously smiled and was heard to say, "I didn't know where I was heading, but here... I have found you... another independent walker." They smiled knowingly at each other... somehow lost in an ancient memory. And so, hand in hand together, feet tapping, they walked further down the road toward another pathway... then dancing. The pathway altered toward another passage downward where there emanated around the bend, yet another seemingly endless "end of a real long road, waiting for some other new friends to come." Dancing into the new distance and into the sounds of that tinny music playing some old Bette Midler song from a jukebox, yes, they found themselves fortuitously in a gay bar. Here, there were women dancing, lots of women. And perhaps T'izm was watching from afar, smiling on our Yu'pik, and too, at Kate, as toes were tapping and women were singing and dancing again. Then with a huge sigh, T'izm walked toward a battered, torn, tattered, and TIMELESS TOME... sighed again... AND CARE-FULLY... yet ever so thoughtfully, and perhaps tenderly, she silently, alone, turned a new page in the Book of Life. And on that page... well... it remains... for you, dear reader... it remains yet to be revealed...

Epoch Eight: In the End...

T'izm was being called back to the Heavens to await the recordings of where she must go next in Time... and under the auspices of that other worldly clock that honored the ticking hands of a more compassionate peace, T'IZM WAS BEING SUBJECTED TO A GREATER GOD. So, with one last healing, because, really, she could not stop herself from bringing this story to a refined completion, and she was first and foremost a Mystic and a Healer...

It was T'izm's decision...

The entirety of these Healing Notations must be handed off to a very special Being. These Healings were meant to be a teaching to a world gone awry.

How now?

T'izm could not ever miss a beat, although she was known to be a procrastinator, but she was getting better. And besides, it was pretty much preordained. It was written in the Recordings of Time and Life and of all Beings of the Light and Dark.

In a moment of Divine clarity, T'izm took a final turn at it and found... Yes... Our Sustanna. Remember, she was Yu'pik's only sister. T'izm, smiling, placed all her notations within Sustanna's reach and gave these precious pages for her to keep, knowing (because remember, T'izm had powers from Beyond, and she intuitively knew many things.) Yes, T'izm knew how to foresee, and it was time to heal those others that the dark Voice of evil had left forsaken in Time. She handed our Sustanna the notations... "Yu'pik's Tale: The Dance."

Intuitively, T'izm understood that Sustanna had greatest ability.

So, she handed the book to our Sustanna with careful advisement to go forward in this life and teach these founding stories. It was known to T'izm that Sustanna remained the only one who could carry this out. And so, it was written in the Book of Life at this point in time that Sustanna, too, in this way, had her life altered. The Mystic T'izm was done for a time and Sustanna, she would go forth and teach the world about these healings.

And I hear you, the reader, asking, "Well, what became of the diminutive Dancer, our 1% Inuit Yu'pik?"

Well, she became the world's greatest dancer, after much practice, and was last seen on a world stage garnering the emotions, through a rhythmic balancing act of not only tapping her feet but also moving the world into greater realms of happiness. Our Yu'pik created waves of happiness that run in the circles of the great ocean tides of love. Finally, those accolades of admiration from all those many women came rebounding from within a much greater following... Yu'pik became, in effect... the best Dancer this world has ever seen.

It's up to you now, dear reader... A mere dance-step? A board game for the imagination? A teaching? Or a Healing? You decide... I know what Yu'pik would say.

It remains that without compassion, there can be no healing.

Yu'pik: "T'izm, you're really not going to go very far away, will you?"

T'izm: "NO."

Yu'pik: "GOOD."

T'izm: "I promised to you, from my heart, we would travel the journey together until... no more."

Yu'pik: "Thank You."

Unfortunately, the beginning of the journey does not often follow the original path to the end.

Epoch Nine: Sustanna's Vision

And it was then that Sustanna stepped forth. She spoke softly to Yu'pik and what She then said, and it was brought about by Her, and this vision WAS all Hers, and it was such as this, "Yu'pik, I have looked deep inside my soul and there beheld a vision of a very young woman being, a woman with a Cheshire smile. Yu'pik, She has come forth. Behold from this hologram before us, I give unto you the Other Worldly Vision of the Sentient Being who will carry you forward now that T'izm is gone." Yu'pik stood there in amazement, staring at the vison of this young woman being within the hologram. She spoke thus, "And who are you?" The young woman released herself from the holds of the hologram and said, "I am Hillary Hers't. I am She who is Healer, and I will be Her, the One who will lead you forward." Turning to Sustanna, Hillary smiled her Cheshire smile and said to Sustanna, "I am now Hers (Yu'pik's), here to heal these wounds."

The hologram then sealed shut as Hillary Hers't, slight of being, special in nature, stepped forward to carry the gauntlet.

Hillary, the being who stepped out of the hologram, takes Yu'pik's hand and walks her through a portal to the future. As she picks up the dusty gauntlet from that dirt road, she hands it over to Yu'pik.

Now, as Yu'pik gets to the other side of that door, there... standing there, also brushing herself off, is T'izm. As Yu'pik stands staring clearly into the soulful eyes of her found Healer, she begins to realize that she has gained a clarity within her spirit and she has regained her spark of life for the living. And Hillary stands there, also staring at the returned Healer, wondering how this will affect her journey with Yu'pik. Remember, dear reader, it was Hillary who first handed Yu'pik that gauntlet, which will now spiritually challenge Yu'pik throughout her life.

And as Hillary began her questionings, quite suddenly, she shattered into a million shards of broken glass. Therein and within each cryptic particle, there grew a tiny seed. Then, suddenly, millions of miniscule holograms exploded about. These holograms held the seeds of new life. These seeds begat the very beginnings of all those who would be known as the Others, those that ever would be, and who would become a newer world ordered by light and compassion. The world as it was now written within the essential self-mending pages of this ancient Tome of Life would become void of all darkness. The miscreant Voice had nowhere else to go. It was consumed.

T'izm smiled and covered herself within her orbed and starry robes. She gathered herself together. She shivered, knowing that winter was coming. A wind was blowing in from the north as Sustanna was beginning a lengthy teaching and had a timely task to accomplish. Sustanna was standing tall as the winds began a shrill howl down the corridors of Time. And Yu'pik, yes, she just danced and became esoterically, most blissfully joyful, mind you, and oblivious to all, except for those who would recognize... the Dance.

It was true, winter was coming. Now the snowflakes were beginning to gather about and bountifully begin to cover the earth and ground. These crystals of frozen ice formations would serve to blanket and warm the frozen earth and herald in the new magic of Spring, like the distant singular callings of winged robins as it would melt when the Others would bring together all those from varied sources and distant shores and arrive.

This is all that is known... and all that is not known.

I know what Yu'pik would say, but better yet, it became all what she did.

She said nothing. Yu'pik danced to the music in her heart. Yu'pik put away all things swarthy and dark.

You, the reader, are given the motions of the Dance. There were no longer any perceptions to be perceived.

STILLNESS...

Epoch Ten: The Final Acknowledgement

And as soon as it all ended... As the glaring hot sun was beating down on that dusty road and eternal pitted pathway, another lone being of the female type could be seen meandering on the passageway and kicking up a filmy haze at the dry dusty soil. She stumbled into what seemed to be a dead body laying quite suddenly still in the middle of the road. It was our Yu'pik. Yu'pik cracked open one solitary eye and spied the female being who was staring most incredulously and in amazement at her, almost laughing. The female being said, "I was walking on this path seeking to save some souls. Hey, I bumped into your body. I thought you were dead. I did not know if rigor had set in, but I see it has not." Yu'pik yawned and stretched amid the confusion and seemed unperturbed with all this new commotion and questioning. She, Yu'pik, then spoke these words, "I was meditating. Hey, and I thought I met the Buddha on the road." And then they both looked quizzically at each other, laughed and said in unison, paraphrasing the Buddhist sage, Linji Yixuan, "If you meet the Buddha on the Road... kill Her." In effect, this means that those who think they found all the answers in any religion, need to start questioning. So, the female said, "Hi, I am called the Dr. I save lost souls. Let us have some tea together and consider this tale of conversion and the Dance." They then peered directly into the center of each other's eyes where their very souls were housed and it was then known that all that had to be known was here and now, in the mindful presence of all the compassionate care surrounding these two.

Yu'pik was about to be healed. The one called the Dr. understood that if you save one soul, you save the world. But it must be accomplished without harm. So Yu'pik accepted all this. This was how the story really ended. It was one Dr., finally, who saved Yu'pik as she acknowledged that a conversion WAS done and that immense trauma had ensued. It was through her sage understanding and her belief in the Hippocratic Oath, that a doctor should do no harm and that it is acceptable to care, that led to the true process of healing for Yu'pik. In spirituality, it remains that only kindness and compassion are the true keys to healing.

And so, these two, Dr. and Yu'pik, sat together as they began to partake in the particulars of a very long story (and a very potent cup of herbal tea) to finalize the healing along with the help of the Others.

And now, this tale from the past brings us through the portal, into the present, and on into the future. I hereby acknowledge Dr. Wong. You are the only ONE from the Others who has finally helped me to put the pieces of my life back together. Thank you ever so deeply from my heart, Dr.

T'izm shivered in the onset of the winter storm...

Sustanna was gathering up the seeds as they floated to the ground... readying to report.

Yu'pik was dancing madly... wildly about, within and without all the newly ordered system of things...

The Dr., waiting in the wings, having reviewed all the progress that Yu'pik had made to this point, was ready to take up her universal role to become the final Healer, as once foretold to the author in a prophetic reading, many years prior. She quietly sipped at her herbal tea and thought all these things through.

Suddenly, all of this activity was brought to a prolific halt in time. The crypt was locked. Hillary, the Guardian of these ancient writings, tucked the key deeply into her makeshift pocket, smiled, and walked away. For it was she who was the keeper of the keys that would ultimately open another door leading to the Others, the Dr., and to the passageway out.

Epoch Eleven

Close-up of a tattered sign over a tainted door of a room of
obsolete design

HILLSIDE PSYCHIATRIC
MEDICAL CENTER
SHOCK TREATMENT ROOM

For Richard, and all those who remain unable to remember what
transpired behind the closed doors of the mental facilities in the
name of accepted medical practice...

Epoch Twelve: Final Vision

At the threshold of the door... a bleeding rose petal, like a broken, bleeding heart... fomenting... a beginning trickling out from the lock... seeds baring tiny holograms falling onto the barren, earthen ground...

Winter had finally come...

Sounds of someone's feet dancing in the distant darkness...

Epilogue

Behind these bizarre events that caused thirty years of frustration and great consternation, the veiled memories with dark angst of the many shadowed miscreant deeds of the dark Voice could not quit until T'izm brought a semblance of organization to the misaligned trace memories and moved them forward into a clarity and a linear format of understanding...

"The Dance" becomes representative of a needed healing from an erroneous belief in the seventies and eighties that expression of homosexuality was in fact a mental disease. The goal in my psychiatric reprogramming was to create an analytic treatment through the use of many psychiatric tools, such as hypnosis, coercion, conversion, operant conditioning, thought implantation, and aversion treatments. These treatments were meant to eradicate my own homophobia and social humiliations, resulting from the social mores of that time. It remains a fact that these resurfacing memories of my conversion, brought about by my treatment with the character only to be known as T'izm, was done through a great space and time difference. We have never met. Our sessions were intense, three times a week, and through

Tele Health discussions, which allowed me a freedom to reveal all the humiliations, hatreds, and basic feelings of shame that surrounded me within my Id's basic drives. These drives, which were thought implantations by the analyst, were meant to bond me to every subsequent therapist, in dysfunction, to hide what the analyst had done.

It also remains a fact that some members of the LGBTQIA+ Community still to this day are considered to be different and not accepted by their parents and society. Not only are they bullied by their peers, but they continue to be bashed and murdered by a societal element that would see them eradicated. Listen, you cannot help but hear the raised voices and the first punch placed at the Riots of Stonewall in June of 1969 that started the Gay Rights Movement. We must never forget Matthew Shepard, who was murdered on October 12, 1998, because he was gay and considered a deviant. May these visions serve as a reminder that we need a massive healing in our souls for what Humankind continues to do to Humankind.

To this day, many of these same people are thrown to the curb, and/or placed into conversion therapy. The object of conversion therapy focuses on converting our "sexual preferences", because homosexuality is **still** believed to be a choice. There are those who would **still** have the world believe that this is not a cellular birthright. Some would continue to perpetrate the idea that we are mutant deviants when, in fact, we are actually born into our sexual identity. Stop and think for a moment. When did you decide to become heterosexual as **your** preference? Do you see how illogical this line of thinking is?

So, now, at seventy-two years of age, I move forward in the Dance of my Life. These conversion tactics bare no soul. THEY WERE WRONG!!! They were set forth by the analyst to destroy all that a greater God once demanded to be put to test. The Mystic T'izm, in this story, puts asunder many of these beliefs and brings the beginning of change. A chance to find healing from Hillary Hers't and the Others has moved Yu'pik's story into the future with the Dr. now leading the way.

You, the reader, have been given the compassionate side of T'izm, the wisdom of Sustanna, the mystery of the hologram bringing forth Hillary, the malfeasance of the Voice, and the recent arrival of an Other, the Dr., and the arduous journey of the one named Yu'pik, the author.

The darkness and heinous acts levied against this author's life during her analytic years from 1982 to 1997 wrought struggles that are now ending and will lead to the true beginnings of a healing journey. Yu'pik and T'izm, who once traveled together, now traverse an altered path. Another road is left to Yu'pik that is currently being explored.

You, the reader, are being invited to traverse this path where you will be offered a time-honored chance, a meeting, to listen to the far - off distant sounds of Yu'pik, the Dr. of the New Order, and the Others, sharing in a healing discussion over one very strong cup of herbal tea.

"Primum non nocere. Secundum cavere. Tertiam sanare." Hippocrates, 460-370 BC

No malfecence. Physician, remember who you are.

The light became the darkness. The darkness became the light.

In the end, it was as in the beginning.

You, the reader, have now been given the Beginning Healings of T'izm, as recorded at this time in the Book of Life, the healing ministering of the Dr., and the resulting **Yu'pik's Tale: The Dance**.

Remember that your freedom is within your heart and mind, and that **no one** should be allowed to take your memories from you. It is through all these memories of all these fighting beings that we stand together!

Remember who you are!

In the final analysis, this book is lovingly handed over to the LGBTQIA+ Community.

e.a. halper

Disclaimer

These writings were written in a fictional, allegorical, mythological style. They hold their basis within a partial reality that began to unfold a long time ago.

If you, the Reader, seek to find or search out any of these beings that are enshrined within these written words, please understand, they do not exist, never existed, and are all themselves non-existent in the real world. You will never be able to find them, nor any remnant of them, except perhaps, in what your dreams are made of. All names held within these pages, for the most part, are fictional and do not represent anyone living or deceased. Such is life, passage is not extended to all. Find your blessings within your heart.

About the Author

e. a. halper is a recently retired advocate for the fragile and emotionally challenged individuals among us. She now resides in New Bern, NC, near her sister, with her companions: her beagle, Marley Star Traveler; Marley's sister; Lucy and Miranda, the betta fish; and the newly adopted Mr. Smitts, the yellow tabby. It remains the author's lifelong dream to continue to advocate for those that society would rather keep hidden away from the light. The truth remains that we only have what we are given at birth and we all, in time, choose the path the universe has intended for us, if the time is right. Once again, e. hopes these writings will reveal a path and a journey in support of all the "children of angst" and the LGBTQIA+ community. And until this malfeasance is eradicated, this author will continue to stand firm in the mindful presence of love!

CPSIA information can be obtained
at www.ICGtesting.com
Printed in the USA
BVHW011428130622
639649BV00006B/391